Other books by Julia Jarman:

New friend
old Friends

Julia Jarman

Illustrated by Kate Pankhurst

Andersen Press · London

First published in 2014 by
Andersen Press Limited
20 Vauxhall Bridge Road
London SW1V 2SA
www.andersenpress.co.uk

2 4 6 8 10 9 7 5 3

Text copyright © Julia Jarman, 2014
Illustration copyright © Kate Pankhurst, 2014
British Library Cataloguing in Publication Data available.

ISBN 978 1 78344 004 7

Printed and bound in Great Britain
by Clays Ltd, St Ives plc

For Faith, Maya, Lois and Ursula, my sparky granddaughters.

Acknowledgements
Huge thanks to Sajida Raza of Sythwood Primary
School, who thought of the title and helped a lot;
to Seherish Ahmed, who showed me how to write
'welcome' in Urdu; to the pupils of Grove Road
Primary School, who advised me on how a *shalwar
kameez* is worn; and to Vimla Randhawa, librarian
at Redbourne Upper School, who checked the
script for howlers.

Daisy

Daisy is friendly and gets on with everyone. She's kind and sensible. She's always thinking of how she can help others and loves being a school 'buddy'. She hates it when people fall out and was very upset when her parents split up, though she's got used to it now.

Phoebe

Phoebe is shy and finds it hard to
make friends. She enjoys craft which
she can do on her own – but it's even
better with Daisy. And Daisy shares her love
of reading. She likes the peace and quiet
of Daisy's house, where they can get on
without being disturbed by Phoebe's
little brothers, the Smellies.

Erika

Erika is entertaining. She's full
of energy and very sporty. She means
well but sometimes doesn't realise she's
hurting people's feelings. She tries very
hard to please her parents who expect
her to be good at everything, and
sometimes that's a strain.

shazia

Shazia is full of fun and very
determined. She has a mind of her
own and this sometimes gets her into
trouble with her parents who have different
ideas. Her family comes from Pakistan.
Shazia is excited about coming to live
in a different country and is keen
to make new friends.

Tuesday

Phoebe

Mrs Davies has chosen *me* to look after the new girl!

I thought she'd choose Daisy because she's a school buddy. Or Erika because she's on the school council. But she chose *me*! I suppose she thought Daisy had enough to do looking out for bullies, and Erika's always busy doing sporty stuff.

The new girl's name is Shazia. I haven't met her yet – she starts on Monday. But I've already been thinking about how I'm going to help her. Mrs Davies says she comes from Pakistan and may not speak much English so I'm going to try and learn some words from her language to help her feel at home. That's *my* idea. I'll find out how to say 'Hello' and 'Welcome to our school.'

Then I'll teach everyone else!

I haven't told Daisy and Erika yet, even though they're my best friends. I'm not sure why I didn't let them know today at school really, but when Mrs Davies told me it felt, well, like a really exciting secret. But she didn't say it was a secret – and they'll be miffed if I don't tell them – so I'll text them both now:

GOT EXCITING NEWS!!! COME ROUND!

I can't stop thinking about it. I mean, I'll have to show Shazia where everything is and make sure she's not lonely and take her to dinners and everything!

Shazia. Sounds like a princess in a fairytale!

Daisy

Phoebe had something really exciting to tell us – a new girl from Pakistan is starting at school. That's near India. Phoebe got out a map and showed us. Mrs Davies has asked her to be the new girl's special buddy and she's taking her job very seriously. *Shazia!* What a lovely name! I'm so looking forward to meeting her. I wonder what she'll be like. Phoebe didn't know much about her, but I hope she'll find out. Phoebe can be rather shy and so might not ask many questions. I wonder what sort of clothes Shazia will wear. Oh, boring thought – she'll probably wear school uniform like everyone else.

Whatever she's like, we'll *all* have to do everything we can to make her feel at home. Actually – I didn't say this to Phoebe – but I'm surprised Mrs Davies didn't ask *me* to look after Shazia. I mean, I'm the one who's a buddy. Anyway I can give Phoebe lots of tips. I'll lend her my *How to Be a Buddy* handbook. And I can teach Shazia playground games and explain about the buddy seat, where anyone can sit if they're feeling lonely.

And – I know! – I'll get Mum to invite her round for some of her Asian cooking! Mum travelled round India and Pakistan when she was a student and picked up some recipes.

I rushed home after Phoebe told us her news and Mum's taught me some Pakistani words already, well Urdu. That's the name of the language they speak, though Mum says they have lots of languages. Just hope it's the right one.

'Hello' is *'Aslam-U-Alaikum'*, 'Yes' is *'Jee'* and 'No' is *'Naheen'*. Sounds quite easy! But that's because they're written down in English the way they *sound.* When they're written down like they would be in Pakistan they use a completely different alphabet.

I'll text them all to Phoebe. Mum says she's sure Shazia will speak good English because in most schools in Pakistan lessons are taught in English.

I wonder if Shazia has brothers and sisters, or whether she's an only child like me.

Erika

Phoebe's news is cool. It'll be great to have another girl in our class. We're outnumbered by the boys at the mo. Hope she's sporty. We're short of players for most of our teams. Mum says Pakistan is famous for cricket and hockey, but she thought only men played sport there.

But she's wrong!

I just Googled Pakistani sports women and they've got a great hockey team and they do squash and gymnastics. In fact a girl called Shazia won a gold medal for gymnastics when she was only eight. Can't be the same Shazia, worse luck, because that was ages ago. Wish it was though. That would be really cool.

It's a pity we don't play hockey at our school – but we will when we go up to seniors – and I'm sure *our* Shazia will want to learn how to play rounders and netball and even five-a-side. I'll teach her the rules. And she can join gym club.

I can't wait to meet her. I hope she speaks English.

Why did Phoebe wait till tonight to tell us? If it had been Daisy or me with news like that we'd have been bursting to tell. She's very secretive sometimes.

Phoebe

Shazia came to school this afternoon and she seems really nice and friendly! It was just for a visit though. She isn't starting school till Monday. She was with her mum and her sister and two little brothers who were ever so naughty! Just like my little brothers!

Our head teacher, Mrs Davies, brought them into our classroom when we were doing art. At first I thought Shazia was the eldest, because she's the tallest, but she isn't. Her sister's going to the senior school. Her brothers are only toddlers, a bit older than the Smellies – that's what I call my little brothers – and they were even more badly behaved than mine!

I couldn't believe it. They chased each other round the classroom, knocking paint pots over, and their mum didn't do *anything*

except look really upset. I think she was worried about her lovely clothes. There was paint flying everywhere. When Shazia and her sister tried to catch the boys they dived under the table in the writing corner and wouldn't come out. Well, not till after Mrs Davies had quickly opened the door and said, 'We'll go and see the library now.'

Even then they waited till their mum was out of sight in the corridor.

Miss Perkins almost slammed the door shut when they'd gone, but it opened again and there was Shazia. She went straight up to Miss Perkins's desk and said, 'I am sincerely sorry about my little brothers. I call them the Monsters and I faithfully promise never ever to bring them to school again.'

Then she walked away with her head bowed – till she reached the door when she turned and gave us all a little wave. I think I managed to catch her eye and give her an encouraging smile – and a wave – because she smiled back, but that may have been to everyone.

I'm longing to tell her about the Smellies and that I completely understand how she feels.

I just wish someone had told me she was coming in today. And it would have been nice if Mrs Davies or Miss Perkins had told Shazia and everyone that it's *my* job to look after her.

Daisy's being very pushy. She managed to say something to Shazia but I don't know what.

And afterwards she told everyone how to say 'Welcome' in Urdu and that was *my* idea!

Daisy

Shazia's going to be really good fun!

Mum was right – she already speaks English so I don't think I'm going to have to use my Urdu. I managed to say *'Kush-amdeed'* though when she shot past my desk trying to catch her little brothers and I think she was pleased.

'Kush-amdeed' means welcome.

Shazia wore really nice clothes – baggy trousers, a long-sleeved tunic top and a scarf. Mum says the outfit's called *shalwar kameez*. It was turquoise and silver and silky and it went really well with her dark hair and skin. And her sandals were silver too. Mind you they had a few red and yellow spots on them when she'd finished chasing after her brothers.

Her mum and sister were dressed in gorgeous clothes too. Her mum had this

gauzy scarf round her shoulders. It had floaty ends with beads on them. I didn't notice what her brothers wore. They spent most of their time under the writing table.

Hope Shazia will do clothes swaps! That would be awesome.

I wonder where they live. I've been keeping a lookout for new people moving in round here, but haven't spotted any removal vans.

Erika

Shazia lives at *my* end of the village!

I saw her going into the flats with her family, all of them even her dad. I rushed out to tell her I lived near and invite her round mine, but by the time I got inside the flats the whole family had disappeared into the lift.

Wish I knew which flat they'd moved in to, or what her surname was. Then I could write her a note and leave it in one of the little post boxes in the entrance.

I'm going to ask her if she'd like to come for a run with me and Rolly. He's my wumply dumply dog. It's light in the evenings now that Spring is here and I want to run as much as I can.

I know, I'll text Phoebe and ask her what Shazia's full name is. Hope she knows.

Shazia looked really agile running between the desks when she was trying to catch her little brothers. Pity about the long trousers and sandals though. If she'd been wearing shorts and a pair of trainers she'd have caught those boys easy peasy.

'We'll have to get her kitted out, won't we, Rolly?'

Oh, I hope she likes dogs.

Phoebe

I don't know Shazia's last name and I wouldn't tell Erika if I did. Oh! Why did I say that? It makes me feel mean. I really do want *everyone* to be friendly to Shazia. It would be awful if they weren't, but . . .

It's just that if Erika gets Shazia doing all that sporty stuff . . . well, she won't have any time left for doing stuff with me and Daisy.

I wish Shazia was living at *our* end of the village – mine and Daisy's – so she could come round our houses and do arty crafty things or Moshi Monsters.

Though, actually, even Daisy's going on as if *she* was Shazia's special buddy. She says her mum is going to invite Shazia round for chapattis, or something. I asked Mum if I could invite Shazia round and she said, 'Not this week, Phoebe! Don't you think I've got enough to do?'

It's because the Smellies are being really difficult at the moment.

Oh. Here's a text from Daisy:

LET'S INVITE SHAZIA FOR A CLOTHES SWAP!

Nice idea, but . . .

There I go again. But it would have to be round Daisy's house, wouldn't it? And I think it's a bit soon for that sort of thing anyway. I mean – will Shazia want to rush round Daisy's house and start trying on our things? I wouldn't want to if I'd just started at a new school.

I'm fed up with Daisy being bossy. *You must do this, Phoebe. You must do that.*

Miss Perkins *still* hasn't told everyone that Mrs Davies asked *me* to look after Shazia.

Daisy

Phoebe's in one of her moods.

I just went round to hers because she hadn't answered my text and her mum said she'd gone to bed early because she was tired. I don't believe her, that she's tired I mean. Phoebe's a night owl. When we have sleepovers she's always the last to go to sleep. She may be in her bedroom, even in bed, but I bet she's not asleep. It's far too early and the Smellies were still running around making a terrible racket.

So what's bugging her?

I can't think of anything I've done. I mean, I've been doing everything I can to *help* her with the new girl.

Oh. Here's a text from Erika.

NEED NEW GIRL'S FULL NAME. PHOEBE NOT ANSWERING. STROP?

Mmm. So Phoebe's not answering Erika, either. But Phoebe doesn't strop. She droops.

I wonder why Erika wants Shazia's full name.

I'm texting Phoebe again.

WHAT'S THE MATTER? TELL ME!

Thursday

Erika

Phoebe *is* in a strop, whatever Daisy says. Well, she *was* for most of the morning. When I got to school and asked her what Shazia's surname was again, she blanked me. She pretended she hadn't heard, but I'm sure she had.

Daisy said Phoebe hardly spoke at all on the way to school and she disappeared at break.

That *is* a strop.

Luckily she cheered up after break, but only when Miss Perkins said, 'Let's have a little chat about the new girl, Shazia, shall we? I know you'll all make her very welcome but, just to make sure she's never left on her own, Mrs Davies has asked Phoebe to be her special buddy for the first few days.'

Phoebe smiled for the first time that day. I think she asked Miss Perkins to say that.

Then Miss Perkins said, 'Let's find out what we can about where Shazia comes from, shall we?'

She got the globe and pointed to a country on the other side of the world.

'Shazia and her family have come all the way from Pakistan which is a country in Asia. She lived in a busy town called Karachi. That's by the sea so she's going to find our village very different.'

She switched on the whiteboard and Googled some photographs of Karachi. It looked VERY different from our village. There was an amazing mix of buildings – high-rise flats and mosques with golden domes, little white flat-roofed houses and towers you could hide Rapunzel in. The traffic was a mix too – huge lorries and little carts pulled by donkeys, swanky cars with dark windows and decorated camels, all jumbled up together with people weaving in and out.

Afterwards I went and asked Miss Perkins if she knew Shazia's family name and she did! It was already in the register.

Her name is Shazia Majeed.

Friday

Welcome

جمعہ ۲ مئی ۲۰

Phoebe

Shazia came into school today – *with Erika!*

When Daisy and I entered the playground Shazia was there, though at first we didn't notice. We just saw Erika with the sporty crowd round her which is quite normal. Then they all drifted across the playground to the netball post and, next thing, Erika was shouting, 'Well done, Shazia!'

And there she was! She'd just scored a goal. We hadn't noticed her at first because she was wearing school uniform just like everyone else, except that she wore trousers, not a pleated skirt like the rest of the girls.

I was so shocked! I didn't know why she was in school today. Why had nobody told me? *I'm* her special buddy.

Daisy said, 'Come on. Let's go and watch

26

– or join in. It's not a match or anything. They're just practising shooting at goal.'

But I didn't feel like it.

Erika and Shazia already looked like best friends. It just wasn't fair. I'd been so excited about meeting Shazia and introducing her to everyone, and Erika had somehow got there first.

But all I said was, 'What are we going to do with our welcome signs?'

We'd made them the night before. Daisy's mum had helped us with the writing. They looked great. But we were going to make more at the weekend.

And we'd practised saying, 'Kush-amdeed.'

Daisy said, 'Let's go into school straight away and put them up just like we planned. I'm sure Mrs Davies will let us.'

I said, 'We can't do *as we planned*, Daisy, because we haven't got enough.' We wanted to put them all over the school.

Anyway, we got permission to go in before the bell and put them up in the classroom. We stuck one on the door so Shazia would see it when she came in, another above the whiteboard so she'd always see it when she was looking at the board and a third in the middle of our table.

Daisy, Erika and I are sitting together this term and there was a spare chair because the girl who used to sit there had left.

I'm beginning to think that's the only reason Mrs Davies chose me – because there's a space.

Anyway, Daisy and I sat down on opposite sides – that was my idea – so that there was an empty seat by each of us.

At least that way Shazia couldn't sit next to Erika.

But she sat next to Daisy, opposite Erika. So they were face to face which was worse. They talked non-stop and they told us that Erika had been round Shazia's house last night and convinced her to start school today!

Shazia did notice the welcome signs and said they were great but that was the only good thing.

Daisy

Phoebe's gone all droopy because she thinks Erika's taking over and trying to be Shazia's special buddy. That's what is bugging Phoebe. But I don't think Erika is. It's just that Erika wants everyone to join in – especially with games and sporty stuff. Erika wouldn't want to do things like show Shazia where to put her coat or where the toilets are.

At lunchtime today I told Shazia that I liked her clothes – the ones she wore when she visited the school. I asked her if she'd like to come round my house and do a clothes swap.

'Clothes swap? What does that mean?'

So I explained how Phoebe and I try on each other's clothes and sometimes borrow them for a while. 'But not school uniform,' I added quickly, thinking of her sparkly turquoise *shalwar kameez*.

Shazia giggled and shook her head and said, 'Sorry, Daisy. My parents would not allow.'

Erika said, 'Why on earth not?' Not that Erika is into swapping, well only trainers and tracksuits and sporty stuff.

Shazia blushed and didn't say anything till Phoebe said, 'It's about . . . modesty, isn't it, Shazia? Your parents wouldn't like you undressing in front of other people.'

Actually Phoebe perked up after that. Because she'd guessed right, I suppose. Anyway, she showed Shazia the drawer where she could keep her books and she helped her with her adverbs in Literacy.

But at break Erika grabbed Shazia's arm and said, 'Come on, let's practise. I think you could be a really good goal attack.'

So Phoebe drooped again.

Actually, I felt a bit droopy too. I wanted to show Shazia my Moshi Monster cards.

Monday

netball

Phoebe

Erika says I've *got* to do something! Just because Shazia wasn't allowed out to play on Saturday! Erika told me she went round to Shazia's on Saturday morning to ask her to come and practise netball, but Shazia's dad wouldn't let her go out. He said she had to stay in and help her mother.

I said, 'Erika, sometimes Mum won't let me go out if she wants help with the Smellies.'

'It's not *sometimes*, Phoebe,' Erika wailed. 'It's always! Her dad said so. Shazia can't stay after school to practise and she can't come out at the weekend. Ever! So she can't be in the team even though she's a brilliant player and we need her. You're supposed to be helping her settle in. Well, she won't, not if she can't *join in*, so go and tell Miss Perkins.'

Miss Perkins is not just our form teacher. She also runs the netball team.

Without waiting for me to reply, Erika shot off – probably to tell Miss Perkins herself.

Then Shazia turned up so I asked her about what Erika had said. To my surprise she seemed even more upset than Erika.

'I *want* to be in the team, Phoebe. I want that very much. I was in the team at my school in Karachi. But I can't.'

Shazia looked as if she was going to cry so I led her to the buddy seat in the playground, and after a deep breath she started to explain.

'In Karachi we lived in a big house with many servants.'

'Servants!' I didn't know anyone with servants.

She nodded. 'Ami-ji, my mother was very happy then and laughed a lot. She helped me and my sister with our homework. We went out to see friends. We had a driver to take us. Another servant looked after the boys. They were nice boys, really cute then. But, Ami-ji, she does not know how to look after little children . . . She's never had to before.'

Shazia's eyes filled with tears so I put my arm round her.

'Now . . .' Shazia continued, 'Ami-ji cries all the time and my brothers run round like racing cars. Hiba, my big sister, she tried to help at first, but now she cries too . . .'

It sounded even worse than my house.

Shazia went on to say it wasn't at all what they expected when they heard that they were coming to England. Mr Majeed said they would have lots of money because he was coming to a good job with International Electronics. He's a computer engineer.

'But it does not seem so much money now because things are so expensive in England. So we live in a tiny flat instead of a big house. We do not have servants and we have only one car.'

I said, 'We've only got one car, Shazia. Daisy's mum hasn't got even one.'

But she didn't seem to hear. She said, 'No aunties, uncles or grandmas, either.' She missed her grandma most of all. She called her Daadi-Ami.

'Daadi-Ami would know what to do,' she whispered. 'But I don't.'

And nor do I!

Daisy

Phoebe has asked me for help but I don't know what we can do except be kind to Shazia at school. I mean we can't get them a big house and servants like they had in Pakistan.

But I did have one idea.

I said, 'Phoebe, does your mum still take the Smellies to a toddlers' group in the community hall?'

She does and they love it. So does Phoebe's mum because she gets to chat with the other mums while the Smellies play on all the equipment. We went with them once and there was a climbing frame and loads of space to charge around. Phoebe's mum said it stopped her going mad.

'And they want more people to go,' said Phoebe, 'or it's going to close down.'

Toddlers' Group is on Tuesday and Thursday afternoons. Tomorrow's Tuesday!

We raced to Phoebe's house after school and persuaded her mum to write a note to Shazia's mum, inviting her to Toddlers' Group. Phoebe's mum even offered to take them and she gave us a leaflet about the group. Then we ran to Erika's to find out exactly where Shazia lived. And we all went round to deliver the note together.

Shazia was ever so pleased to see us. She said, 'Come in quickly' because she had to close the door to stop the Monsters running out.

Then we all trooped into the sitting room to give Shazia's mum the note, and Phoebe explained why we'd come really well. I was very proud of her.

But then Shazia's mum shook her head!

I couldn't believe it. It was *so* disappointing. There we were with a really helpful suggestion and she said, *'Naheen.'* No!

But then Shazia's dad came home from work and Shazia showed him Phoebe's mum's note and the leaflet, and he said, 'I think this is a very good proposal, Raheela. The hand of friendship is being offered and you must accept. You must go.'

Talk about bossy!

Erika

We all high-fived when we got outside.

Phoebe and Dais were well pleased that their plan to help was working. But I still wasn't sure it would help me get a team together for the match against St Swithins. We really needed Shazia as goal attack.

Dais thought it might help in the long run. She said, 'If Shazia's mum cheers up and starts learning how to look after little kids, then Shazia might be allowed to come out a bit more.'

So it was Operation Cheer Up Shazia's Mum.

I'm going to ask my mum to invite her round for coffee or a cup of tea. Trouble is, Mum's so busy. Just hope she's got a day off work coming up soon.

At least Shazia can still practise in school time.

wednesday

Phoebe

I have to admit it's great having Daisy and Erika to help. Erika's mostly helping so Shazia can be in the netball team, but I see now that would make Shazia ever so happy.

And Daisy's idea about Toddlers' Group was a brainwave. It went really well. Luckily yesterday was a nice Spring day. Mum says they opened the doors of the community hall so there was even more space outside. The Monsters and the Smellies raced round on ride-ons. The Monsters were a bit wild at first, Mum says, but that's because they've been cooped up in a flat without a garden. There was only one panic, at the end, when they couldn't find the Monsters. But – after a lot of searching – they found them under the stage where the ride-ons are stored!

Afterwards Mum took them to the playing fields next to our school. We saw them when we came out, scrambling over the climbing frame like monkeys. Well, the boys were! Our mums were sitting on a bench chatting.

Mum says Shazia's mum seems rather sad – everything is new for her and she's a bit overwhelmed and lonely – but Mum thinks getting out of the house will help.

At school today Shazia said the Monsters nearly fell asleep over their supper last night *and* when they were put to bed they stayed there *and* they slept the whole night through. Her mum didn't shout or cry at breakfast and she says she's going to take the boys to Toddlers' Group tomorrow.

The other exciting bit of news today is that there's going to be an extra school disco. In assembly Mrs Davies said that we need to raise funds for new books for the library.

I just hope Shazia can come to the disco.

Daisy

Do hope Shazia will be allowed to come to the disco. I think there's a good chance if she isn't needed at home so much. Shazia says her dad is really strict, but he seemed really nice – bossy and serious but nice – and sensible! A bit like me really!

Well, he was sensible about Toddlers' Group.

I'm sure Shazia can persuade him to let her go – if Operation Cheer Up Shazia's Mum is a success. It's got to be. Idea! I'll get Mum to invite them all round for that meal she promised to cook. We can talk about the disco, and how important it is to raise money for new books.

And I'll show Shazia my disco dancing gear!

Monday

Phoebe

Daisy has blown it! She's undone all our good work!

Daisy got her mum to invite the Majeeds round on Saturday – good – but then she paraded in her disco gear – *bad*! She actually came downstairs in her short skirt and skimpy skinny top! I mean how could she be so stupid? I'd explained about modesty when Shazia said she couldn't do clothes swapping. I explained all about different cultures with different ideas of right and wrong. I told her bare shoulders and legs were out – or rather not out.

But she hasn't apologised!

She says that it was all going well with the grown-ups sitting round after the meal being chatty. Mr and Mrs Majeed were saying how delicious her mum's food was. Then her

mum started telling them about the PTA and fundraising. Hiba, Shazia's sister, was keeping an eye on the Monsters, so Daisy said, 'Let's go upstairs, Shazia. I'll show you my disco gear.'

Today at school I said, 'Shazia, why didn't you stop Daisy going downstairs to show your parents?'

She said, 'I was in her home, Phoebe, and in her home she is doing what she wants to do. And my parents too they think people in their own homes do – how do you say? – do their "own thing".'

'But they went very quiet Daisy says.' Daisy *had* noticed that.

Shazia said, 'Yes, they were shocked, but they didn't say anything. That would be very impolite.'

'But they went home soon afterwards.'

'Only because they needed to put my brothers to bed.'

'But they won't let you go to the disco now.'
I felt sure.

But Shazia wasn't sure. 'I have not asked them yet. I am waiting for the right time. Life is better now that your mother has befriended my mother. I think they will let me go, if I wear my own clothes. I am . . . working on it.'

Then she giggled. 'Phoebe, I *loved* Daisy's disco clothes. I *did* try them on you know.'

I was speechless. What if her parents had come upstairs?

Erika

Daisy is crazy!

I mean, did she really think Shazia's mum and dad would like her disco clothes?

And Phoebe is being very *pheeble*! She is sure there's nothing we can do to persuade Shazia's mum and dad to let her come out more. But I'm not giving up. Not yet. Not when, with a bit of effort, we can save the day. I'm sure we can.

Another thing, Phoebe says that Shazia's dad will never ever let her play in matches, because he'll never ever let her wear shorts. But she doesn't have to! I've noticed that some teams play in tracksuit bottoms. So Shazia could too!

I'm going to ask Miss Perkins and I'm sure she'll agree. I mean, Shazia wears trousers for school anyway. In fact – just thought of this –

I'm going to put it to the school council that all girls can wear trousers if they want to. I mean, it's all right at the mo, but in Winter our legs get freezing. Trousers would be much more sensible.

Two problems solved – well almost!

I'd better see Miss Perkins first thing tomorrow. In fact I'll ask her to phone Shazia's dad and try and persuade him to let her play in the match on Wednesday, wearing a tracksuit.

Tuesday

Daisy

Hooray!!

Shazia can go to the disco! And she can play in the match on Wednesday. Miss Perkins phoned her dad and persuaded him. Shazia told us all at school today. But only if she wears her *shalwar kameez*. For the disco not the match! Her father says she can't wear disco clothes and he has a special reason for wanting her to wear her traditional dress that night.

I said, 'That's fine, Shazia. Is it a special festival or something?'

Shazia said she didn't think it was, because if it was she'd have to stay at home and go to the mosque with her family.

I said, 'Really, Shazia, you'll look lovely.'

But she pulled a face. 'I've been thinking about it. I don't want to be the only one not wearing disco clothes. I want to look like you,

Daisy. I want to dance like you and everyone else and I cannot do that in a *shalwar kameez*. So this is my plan . . .'

She said she'd go to the disco in her traditional dress, and swap with me when she got there – because she knew how much I wanted to try on her *shalwar kameez*. Then we would change back again before the end, ready for when her mother or father met her.

I said, 'So I'd get to wear your *shalwar kameez*?'

'Only if you really want to, Daisy.'

I *do* want to, but, well, I wasn't sure about her plan. Was it too risky? What if we got caught?

I said, 'Your parents would be furious if they found out. They'd never trust you afterwards. You'd never ever be allowed out again. And they would be cross with me too.'

It would be the end of Operation Cheer Up Shazia's Mum for sure.

Shazia said, 'They won't find out. I will change back into my own clothes before the end of the disco.'

I said, 'Let's discuss this with Phoebe first – and Erika.'

Erika would be furious – with me! – if Shazia was grounded and couldn't play in her precious netball team. As for Phoebe, well, she'd never forgive me if I didn't tell her about this.

But Shazia didn't want me to tell them.

'Erika is – how do you say it? – a blabber mouth? She is sure to tell someone. And Phoebe, lovely Phoebe, it would worry her very much.'

'It worries *me* very much.'

Shazia laughed. 'No, you like adventures, Daisy.'

I said, 'In books, Shazia.'

She giggled and linked her arm in mine. 'We will be in *disguise*. It will be exciting.'

Shazia's so fun! And if she's willing to take the risk, shouldn't I be braver too? Suddenly it *seemed* very exciting. I pictured myself in her gorgeous *shalwar kameez* . . .

Shazia put her finger over her lips. 'This will be our secret, Daisy.'

Phoebe

Shazia isn't so chatty at the moment, not to me, except about netball and I don't care about stupid netball. I'm pleased she's going to play for the team today but I don't want to hear all about 'Wonderful Erika' arranging everything.

And Erika's going round as if she's won the lottery.

But Daisy's behaving even more strangely. She's been really odd all week. She's gone all quiet. I haven't had a proper goss with her for days. And we usually talk lots about what we're going to wear when there's a disco coming up. I know I had a go at her about last Saturday night but I'd have thought she'd have got over that by now.

If it were anyone else I'd assume they were

just in a mood. But Daisy doesn't have moods – well, not like I do. She can't bear to be on bad terms with anyone for long.

And she *is* talking to Shazia – a lot. I heard them talking about the disco, but they stopped when they saw me.

It's as if they're plotting something.

Daisy

I've changed my mind.

I've been trying to persuade Shazia not to go ahead with it, but she's determined. I've never met anyone so determined, well, except Erika when she's in a race. Perhaps that's why those two get on so well. And they get on even better now Shazia's in the netball team.

But Erika would *not* like Shazia's plan. Nor would Phoebe and I think she's getting suspicious. At break today she said, 'What are you going to wear for the disco, Shazia?'

The three of us were in the playground. Well, I held my breath, wondering what Shazia would say, when Erika breezed out on her way to the games area.

'Come on, Shazia. Let's practise!'

As the two of them ran off across the

playground Phoebe looked like a hurt kitten, then a suspicious kitten.

I said, 'Sporty types, eh?' I tried to laugh it off, but Phoebe looked at me with her eyes scrunched up.

'Do you know what Shazia is wearing for the disco, Daisy? Is that what you've been whispering about?'

Well, I felt myself going red. Honestly, I wanted to tell her. I was longing to talk it over with her, but I'd promised Shazia I wouldn't.

Sort of promised. I hadn't actually *said* I wouldn't. But Shazia thought I had.

Phoebe persisted. 'You know, don't you? She's up to something and you know what her plan is.'

Well, I didn't say anything, but my tummy was squirgling and all sorts of thoughts were going round in my head. *It was right to tell Phoebe. It was wrong. I'd upset Shazia if I did. Shazia might be in big trouble if I didn't.*

Phoebe was still staring at me.

I said, 'Can you keep a secret?'

Thursday

Erika

We won 5–0 yesterday and Shazia scored three of our goals!

Her dad picked us up after school and when we arrived at their flat her mum met us with garlands of flowers which she put round our necks. Her little brothers clapped. They were quite sweet in fact. I felt as if I'd won at the Olympics.

Tea was delicious, spicy but not too hot and I ate *loads*.

After tea her dad said, 'Why don't you show Erika your best *shalwar kameez* that you are wearing for the disco, Shazia? Go to your bedroom and put it on.'

When Shazia came back I didn't know what to say.

The outfit was my favourite colour, purple, and had silver and gold embroidery and matching slippers. Dais and Phoebe would have drooled and gasped, 'Gorgeous'. They love girlie things, the silkier and sparklier the better, but it wasn't really my style.

'Well, what are you thinking?' said Mr Majeed. 'Do you not think all the girls will want an outfit like that?'

I said, 'Yes. It's lovely. Daisy would swap like a shot if she had the chance.'

But mentioning Daisy obviously wasn't a good idea. Shazia's eyes opened wide and she shook her head frantically.

Mrs Majeed said, 'What will you be wearing for the disco, Erika?'

'Not sure yet,' I replied. It was true. I mean the disco wasn't till the weekend. I said, 'I've had more important things on my mind recently, like the match – and my school work.'

I could almost hear Daisy saying, 'Creep' as I said that, but it was exactly the right thing to say.

Mr Majeed thought I was great. 'You are very sensible, Erika. I am glad that Shazia has a sensible friend. I hope you will both enjoy the disco.'

Shazia said, 'I'm sure we will. Thank you, *Abu-ji*.'

She sounded like a really good little girl, but then she winked at me. *What* was that about?

Phoebe

I can't believe what Daisy and Shazia are planning to do on Saturday!

I said, 'Daisy, you can't. It's crazy.'

Then she said, 'I know. But . . .'

'But what?'

'Shazia's so keen to fit in and . . .'

'And?'

'And she's so excited about it and she trusts me. Please don't tell her I told you, Phoebe. I don't want to let her down. You know how unhappy she was before this and she's quite sure her parents won't find out and . . .'

'And?' I was still waiting for a really good reason.

Daisy sort of smiled. 'It could be really good fun, Phoebe. Please help us.'

'How?'

'By not breathing a word.'

Daisy explained how they were going to do the swap. 'Shazia will arrive in her *shalwar kameez*. I'll arrive in my disco gear. As soon as we're sure our parents have gone we'll dive into the toilets and change.'

I said, 'What about changing back, Daisy? Remember Cinderella? *Dong! Dong! Dong!* She forgot the time.'

'Good point,' she said. 'That's something you could do – keep an eye on the clock. If we swap back a good quarter of an hour before the end of the disco, we'll be in our own clothes well before the parents arrive to pick us up.'

I said, 'Half an hour would be better. What if they come early?'

'Another good point, Phoebe!' Daisy hugged me. 'I feel much better now you've agreed to help.'

I didn't realise I had!

Erika

The disco's tomorrow night and something's up.

Last week Dais and Phoebe weren't speaking. This week they've been whispering all the time. But they're not exactly best friends. At break today I heard Daisy snap, 'NO, Phoebe. How many times do I have to tell you?' But they wouldn't tell me what they were arguing about.

Daisy said, 'It's just a little surprise we're planning.'

I think it's about the disco and that Shazia's in on it too. Sometimes the three of them are in a huddle.

Phoebe looks really miserable though.

Another thing. Neither of them has asked me what I'm wearing, which is odd because they usually inspect what I'm going to wear several days before. I think they worry I'd go in my tracksuit if they didn't. And after school when Shazia came round mine – to practise at goal I thought – she wanted to practise *dancing*.

Well, I did my best to show her some steps but I wasn't really in the mood. It might have helped if she'd told me what was going on, but when I asked her she just giggled.

I've a good mind not to go to the stupid disco.

Saturday

Daisy

It went wrong, horribly horribly wrong!

I should have listened to Phoebe. There wasn't a single hour yesterday when she didn't say, 'Are you sure about this, Daisy?' And I snapped back at her every time, 'Yes!'

But I wasn't really. I had my doubts all along. Even though Shazia's excitement was catching, and I was so excited about wearing her *shalwar kameez*.

I did ask Shazia several times if *she* was sure, and she said, 'Yes, I am certain. Please, Daisy, this is my big chance to be like everyone else, and you know you want to wear my *shalwar kameez*.'

Luckily she didn't mind that I'd told Phoebe, not when I explained why.

It started off OK. Phoebe and I arrived at

school just before six o'clock. I was wearing my sparkly blue skirt and my silver top. Phoebe was in her shimmery rainbow-coloured skirt and top. We'd walked to school on our own, but Phoebe's dad was going to pick us up at eight o'clock when the disco ended. Loud music was already coming from the school hall and it wasn't long before the doors opened.

We waited in the entrance till Shazia and Erika arrived. We knew Erika's mum was dropping them off. Then Shazia and I shot into the toilets and changed. I *adored* wearing her beautiful *shalwar kameez*. It made me feel so special and I couldn't stop looking at myself in the mirror.

But Shazia gasped when she saw herself in my clothes again. The skirt looked even shorter on her because she has long legs. Then she giggled and said, 'Come on, Daisy.'

She almost dragged me into the hall. The

curtains were closed so it was dark except for the disco lights flashing.

'What the . . .?' said Erika when she saw us. For a few minutes she was speechless. Then she said, 'You do realise this could ruin everything, Daisy? *Everything.*'

I said, 'Shut up.' But I don't think anyone

else heard.

Several girls near enough to see said we looked great.

Phoebe looked worried. She hardly danced all evening. I don't think her eyes left the clock in the hall. But even that didn't stop things going wrong.

Phoebe

All I can say is that I did my best, but DISASTER STRUCK!

Mr Majeed arrived at seven o'clock, *a whole hour* early!

I saw him first because I was standing near the door to the entrance hall, looking up at the clock which was just above it. He came in and scanned the room looking for Shazia. I saw him think he'd spotted her at the back of the hall and take a step towards the middle of the room – *towards Daisy*. With the disco lights flashing, all he could see from the door was the sparkles of the *shalwar kameez*, not who was wearing it.

Oh no. I held my breath.

I thought he was going to walk over right then, but he must have thought better of trying to make his way through all the bopping bodies because he stopped and looked around for a teacher.

My breath came out in a spurt as I realised I had to warn Shazia. Warn them both. Where was Shazia? If I could get to them before Mr Majeed, they might have time to get to the toilets and change their clothes.

Now Mr Majeed was talking to Mrs Davies, who was looking straight at Daisy. Oh no. She started striding towards her, and dancers parted to let Mrs Davies through. Could I get to Daisy first?

No one stood aside to let *me* through. The hall had never seemed so long, or the bodies so close together, as I weaved in and out of the dancers, with the music drumming in my ears. But at last I reached Daisy.

Just before Mrs Davies.

I hoped Shazia had escaped to the toilets.

Daisy

Suddenly I felt my arm being tugged.

Phoebe was hissing in my ear. 'Daisy, go to the toilets . . .'

Mrs Davies stood just behind her and was bellowing, 'Shazia, I'm sorry but . . .' Luckily she couldn't see my face because Phoebe was in the way.

'Toilets!' Phoebe hissed again. 'Swap back with Shazia!'

'Your father is here . . .' shouted Mrs Davies.

I saw him, Mr Majeed, at the side of the hall, and realised the danger.

I ran across the hall, out into the lobby, then into the toilets, where I hoped Shazia was waiting.

'Shazia!' I yelled at the cubicle doors.

No reply.

'Have you seen Shazia?' I asked a couple

of girls who were gathered round one of the mirrors.

They shook their heads.

I turned as the main door opened.

'Shazia?'

But it was Phoebe looking as if she was being pursued by a raging monster.

'Is . . . Sha—?' She could hardly get the words out.

'No,' I shook my head and dived into a cubicle as the door opened again and there stood Mrs Davies.

'Girls, what's the matter?'

Phoebe – I don't know how she thought of it – said, 'Shazia's upset, Mrs Davies. She put a bit of make-up on and she thinks her father will be angry.'

There was a silence. Then Mrs Davies said, 'Well, tell her to wipe it off quickly and come out. Her father is waiting.'

I heard the door close and thought, *What do we do now?*

Erika

As soon as I saw Shazia in Daisy's disco skirt and top I knew something would go disastrously wrong and it did.

I'll never forgive them for not telling me what they were up to. Never. And Dais is the one who prides herself on being so sensible!

I can't forget the moment Shazia realised her dad was in the room. One minute we were dancing in a group with a few others. Next she stopped suddenly, her arms in midair.

I said, 'What's up?'

But she didn't reply. She just turned round and shot off, dodging between all the moving bodies. Did she need the loo in a hurry? I looked round – and saw Mr Majeed standing by the door.

And there was Phoebe staring up at him, looking white and shaky.

Catching on, I looked in the opposite direction. Well, Shazia wouldn't have rushed into her furious father's arms, would she? I couldn't see her in the dark, but I headed for a door on the other side of the hall. Was she in the corridor?

No.

What now?

I opened one of the classroom doors leading off the corridor and called out, 'Shazia, come out! It's me, Erika. Let's find Daisy and swap back before your dad sees you.'

No reply.

Well, I must have looked in every classroom – the corridor went right round the hall – till I found myself back in the lobby. I was behind Mr Majeed and Mrs Davies who were talking to each other.

The front door was open. Could Shazia have run out past them?

But where to?

As I stood behind the grown-ups I heard Mr Majeed say, 'I am bringing such a very nice surprise for Shazia. Her grandmother has arrived from Pakistan for a holiday. That is one of the reasons I wanted her to wear her very best *shalwar kameez*.'

Then the door to the toilets opened and two girls came out. Through the open door I saw Phoebe beckoning frantically and I dashed inside.

Phoebe whispered, 'Go and get Shazia. Daisy's ready to swap back.'

I whispered, 'Can't. I've looked all over the school. She's disappeared.'

Phoebe

I felt terrible. I mean, I was supposed to be looking after Shazia.

I said, 'She must be somewhere.'

But where? I started to rack my brains.

Erika said, 'Where's Daisy?'

'Here,' mumbled Daisy from behind the cubicle door, 'And here's the *shalwar kameez*.' A bundle appeared under the door. 'Listen. We've got to find Shazia. It's best if we all look. Can you find me something to wear?'

All I could see was a bin bag, lining the bin. Luckily there were only a few tissues in it.

'Sorry, Daisy, it's all I can find,' I said as I shoved it under the door. I pushed the *shalwar kameez* back too. 'You'd better hide this under it.'

Honestly, when she came out . . . Any other time Erika and I would have laughed ourselves silly, but there was too much to do. I'd had a hunch where Shazia might be. I could hear her voice saying, *'This would be very good for a game of hide-and-seek.'* Where were we when she'd said that?

Suddenly I remembered – on the playing field after Toddlers' Group, when my mum told us about how the Monsters got stuck *under the stage* where they keep the ride-on toys in the village hall.

Would she hide there?

It was the only place I could think of so we made a plan.

Daisy

When Mrs Davies saw me step into the lobby her mouth fell open.

Erika said, 'Dais has spilled Coke all over her new clothes, Mrs Davies. She thinks she should go home and put them in the washing machine straight away.'

Mrs Davies frowned. 'And Shazia?' She looked at Phoebe. 'Is she er . . . ready?'

'Nearly,' said Phoebe breezily. 'She'll be out in a minute.'

Mr Majeed was laughing as we edged towards the door. 'I do hope Shazia does not want to be wearing the latest bin-bag fashion. Her Daadi-ami would not approve.'

Mrs Davies was still frowning. 'Girls . . .'

I think she was going to say we shouldn't be going home alone. Or question us about Shazia. But it was too late. We were outside.

I just hoped she wouldn't go into the toilets and look for Shazia – or come after us.

Phoebe strode ahead. When we got out of sight of the school we ran.

Luckily the village hall wasn't far – it took us about three minutes to reach it – and the door was open. We could hear grunts and gasps from the badminton players as we stood in the entrance. When Phoebe opened the door to the main hall we saw shuttlecocks flying around.

Nobody stopped us as we crept round the sides of the hall to the stage. We had excuses ready – we were looking for the bag Phoebe's mum had left at Toddlers' Group – but no one asked.

So everything went smoothly.

Except that Shazia wasn't under the stage.

Erika

So much for Phoebe's amazing hunch!

As we removed the panel at the front to reveal tractors and tricycles and a ride-on turtle, I prayed Shazia would crawl out.

She didn't.

Daisy called Shazia's name, but there was no answer.

She whispered, 'Come out, Shazia, if you're in there. We've got your *shalwar kameez*. If we move fast we might be able to get you back to school and er . . .'

She didn't say what the rest of her plan was.

Daisy crawled under the stage – and out again. We all helped put the panel back.

As we walked out of the hall the badminton match ended.

A lady called out, 'Find what you wanted, girls?'

Phoebe shook her head. I think she was close to tears. I was desperate for the loo.

Apologising for delaying the others, I dived into the ladies'.

And there was Shazia, crouched in a corner!

Phoebe

I was nearly right!

It didn't take long to get Shazia out of Daisy's disco clothes and into her *shalwar kameez*. Daisy put her own clothes back on and went to shove the bin-bag in the waste bin but I stopped her.

'We need that.'

We raced back to the school gate and hid behind the wall, where we could see Mrs Davies and Mr Majeed in the entrance.

Now for the hard bit – getting Shazia inside without arousing suspicion.

'Hitch up your *shalwar*, Shazia.' I meant her trousers. Then I put the bin-bag over her head, covering her completely.

Daisy and I took hold of her arms and we led her to the door.

Erika stayed behind the wall.

Of course Mrs Davies looked up as we got near the door. So did Mr Majeed.

'What on earth . . .?'

They both looked confused, but laughed, which is what we wanted. We were ready to say it was Erika trying out the new bin-bag fashion but we didn't need to. We dived into the toilets and whipped the bin-bag off Shazia, who rushed out again and into her father's arms.

'Abu-ji! Did I hear you say Daadi-ami is here? Let's go home *now!*'

Mrs Davies went into her room and we hurried into the hall. After a few minutes Erika joined us and we had a massive group hug.

Phew!

Friday

A Week Later

Shazia

The minutes that I passed in the village hall seemed like hours. Soon I wished that I had not panicked and run away from the disco. But I knew Abu-ji would be angry to see me in the disco clothes, because I had disobeyed and deceived him. That is why I ran – right out of the school and into the village hall. But then I did not know what to do, till my new friends found me.

Wonderful friends! Daisy and Phoebe and Erika helped me so much.

I have not seen them quite as often this week, not after school, because I am spending time with my darling Daadi-ami. But next week it is clubs and teams once again and on Saturday afternoon I am doing Hula Hoop Club with my three best friends.

Daadi-ami is happy that I have such wonderful friends.

We are like the Famous Five. There's Daisy, Phoebe, Erika, me and Rolly the wumply dumply dog!

make friends BREAK friends

Julia Jarman

Daisy has two best friends, Phoebe and Erika,
but they don't get on. Erika thinks Phoebe's feeble
and Phoebe thinks Erika's a bully. Daisy has a plan
to get her two best friends to like each other, but
suddenly everyone is against her! Then the three
girls have to spend a night together in a spooky
old mill . . .

'Entertaining and realistic'
Julia Eccleshare, Lovereading

Gorgeously illustrated
throughout by Kate
Pankhurst.

9781849395090 £4.99